SOAKING IN STRANGE HOURS

A Tristan Grieves Fragment

ERIK HOFSTATTER

Copyright (C) 2021 Erik Hofstatter

Layout design and Copyright (C) 2021 by Next Chapter

Published 2021 by Next Chapter

Edited by Ashley Conner

Cover art by CoverMint

This book is a work of fiction. Names, characters, places, and incidents are the product of the author's imagination or are used fictitiously. Any resemblance to actual events, locales, or persons, living or dead, is purely coincidental.

All rights reserved. No part of this book may be reproduced or transmitted in any form or by any means, electronic or mechanical, including photocopying, recording, or by any information storage and retrieval system, without the author's permission.

For you, laguna soul

Unblinking stars chaperoned me to the dockyard where I drank with old ships. The world was more bearable at midnight. No soul-eaters masquerading as people.

Dark Horse raced to my hands. A cheap title printed across a flask once given to me by a writer I've never met. I disliked his book, but his generosity tasted good on my lips. When ghost faces of abandoned loves scream at your heart, a stranger's benevolence can keep you alive for a little longer.

The whiskey sang to a tired audience built from my veins. I listened.

"Are you lost?"

"And now I'm found."

We sat on a bench, commemorating someone who no longer mattered. I looked at her face. Moonlight suited her. It erased sins of wild youth. She moved closer. I smelled like poverty. Unwashed hair and unwashed soul. Wars were lost inside my eyes.

"What's your name?" she said.

"Tristan Grieves."

"I'm Liene."

Her ear was small and naked. In the other, she wore an earring—a dangling feather. I knew Liene was the kind of woman other women desperately tried to imitate, but how could you dress in someone else's charisma? She had a style that spoke without an eccentric accent. A footprint that provoked curiosity in men like me.

"You soak in strange hours, Liene."

"Whilst you just soak in alcohol."

"I'd rather soak in you."

She moved even closer. Her eyelashes were strong and thick, like little whips.

"You want to taste me?"

Whiskey devils blurred my vision. I thought about gullible

lovers, climbing those words all the way up to her clever lips. Then how they fell and died when she spat them out.

"Maybe under a different moon, darling."

Her laugh belonged to a lying child, but she stayed close to me. Cold fingers slept in my lap. I was a fool for white poison, two decades younger.

"So what brought you here tonight?" Liene said.

"I like drinking with wooden bodies. You?"

Mischief traveled in her eyes, gaining speed as she unsealed a little plastic bag.

"I bury my problems under a naughty avalanche. You want some?"

She read *no* in my face, but held her gaze anyway. There was something behind those eyes—a dirty innocence etched on hypnotic, pale-blue amulets. I watched her nose hoover borrowed happiness. Swans painted black by the night watched her, too.

"We wear the same heart bruises, you know."

I heard a ball of accent hopping on that word roulette. Her tongue had a passport to many places.

"Tell me about your origin," I said.

Liene slouched. The weight of my question seemed too heavy for her. I waited. Above our heads, cloud bullies mocked us in their own way.

"I'm an English soul stranded in a Czech body."

Even her phrasing brand walked tall on the language catwalk. I rode on her pheromone thunder, feeling electric. I drank more whiskey and thought about her eyes.

"What are you thinking about?"

"I'm thinking about your eyes."

"Are you drowning?"

"In big blue ice cubes, yeah. I want to meet them at the bottom of a whiskey glass."

I sold shares in grim insights, and she still paid in smiles. I watched her mouth—a cocaine-white theater of teeth.

"I read somewhere that hell is the eyes of a lost lover," she said.

"Is that why your nose orbits planet coke? You lost someone?"

"No, Tristan. I was his hell."

Her revelation nudged me off the bench. I lived on a past diet of hellish women. I gambled with fate and its petty love torments. I lost tears and hair and quarter of my weight to them.

"Where are you going?"

"Emigrating to quieter benches."

Drunk feet and sober instinct carried me away from that crazy bullet. I walked in hungry puddles and still felt like they were richer than me.

"Wait."

I was arrested by the cry of need. Something in her voice had the power to command—to destroy. She moved with feline confidence, her hips narrating trouble.

"What do you want from me, Liene?"

"The tiniest vial of your help."

A vagabond fox trespassed on her shadow. For one night, they shared colors. Maybe even lies.

"Help with what?"

Those vixen eyes, spinning my every thought. I smelled her faux fur coat scented with opium and porn-star dreams. She wished to be fucked, wearing nothing but that coat.

"You think I like to be dressed in sweat of strangers?"

"It's cold, and I like to keep my throat warm with a whiskey scarf."

The flask was dry, so I drank her old words. *The tiniest vial of your help*. Typing on red enigma, I felt tired, helpless in my own skull-sized hell.

"Come to my place," she said. "If you lend me your ears, I'll pay you in booze."

"Where do you live?"

"I live in-between hearts."

"Sorry?"

"You know, somewhere on that fracture line when a heart is about to break."

She was higher than a suicide bridge, but the mud on her soul had my handprint in it. Moth soldiers partied hard under streetlights, and I wanted to eat their spirit.

Liene finger-stabbed my shoulder.

"Oi. Daddy Moth. Your fire is here."

My heart—a survivor of third-degree burns, even when days still smelled like fire-daughters.

I touched my chest and imagined a human pump—charred and ugly, slaving in a hospice for dying organs.

"Wrong night for a heart attack, man."

"Hope you brought croc tears." I said, waiting for a reaction that never arrived.

The weather turned, and God spat in our faces.

"Where's your den again?"

"On the other side of Luton Arches. Walk with me?"

Three words, hundred interpretations—all ballads for undefeated sinners.

I weighed my temptation and lost to the hurricane caged inside of her.

"Course. I got nothing to lose and nothing to drink."

"That logic is packing flavor." Liene held my hand.

It was tattooed with scars and rain.

———

We stood in someone else's misfortune. A shelter for the homeless. Her eyes alone were a soundtrack to this funeral of egos.

Identities trashed in unclean bodies on concrete beds. Living on knees in a world that nullified them. I wondered if impetuous decisions would total me a zero, too, someday.

"It'll start raining soup in a minute,"

Liene crushed half a cig under her heel. An old street lord picked it up as we walked away. I watched smoke eat the grief from his face in a city the color of gargoyles.

"Why do you linger among undesirables?" I said.

"Why do you?"

"I'm one of them."

She told me the stairs were once caressed by fire and Russian feet. A redhead hooker guarded locks to her flat. There was something animalistic carved into her aura.

"Why is she modeling semen shampoo on your doorstep?"

"Katerina? She's got claws, man."

I followed her inside. The wallpaper looked like it contracted hepatitis years ago. I sauntered on a carpet pregnant with red wine stains and bad memories. She shrugged off her coat and lit a candle—held by the mouth of an absinthe bottle. A guitar born in a faraway Spanish region caught my eye.

"Do you play?"

"Only when I'm sad."

Poetry books that once slept rough on cold shelves. Skulls and forever roses. Age-old trinkets bought in cobblestone cities. I recognized the language of a passionate woman.

"What are you thinking about?" she said.

"Something I once read."

"Tell me."

"A passionate woman is worth the chaos."

"And do you think I'm worth the chaos?" She handed me a glass of unbranded whisky.

"I think your chaos would bury my heart at the bottom of the Nile."

Liene showed me the white river flowing between her teeth.

Her eyes narrated fog-clad riddles, and in winter, sparred naked with skinny intellects. I saluted her.

"Thanks for the amber bribe. Why am I here?"

"I want you to find someone."

Drinking bought me time but not clarity. I knocked back a shot. Then we both sank into her chesterfield three-seater. It was beaten by strong hands of previous masters. So was she.

"What do you mean? I avoid people. I don't look for them."

"No, but you look for forgiveness."

"And I'm not gonna find it here." I felt distraught by her acute temperament.

We were empty crosswords, searching each other's minds for missing letters. I could never guess hers.

"Then help me find mine." Liene got up and walked for a beer.

The shape of her ass was still pressed in the leather. I thought about angles and reasons and cocooned agendas. Maybe I was another sad guitar she wanted to play.

"His name is Boomerang," she said, twin bottles in hand.

I adopted one and gave it a home in my mouth. It tasted like a burned-down bohemian orphanage.

The inked fool on her shoulder spoke to me. I was often neck-deep in tarot meanings when night undressed the moon.

"Come back," she said.

"Yeah, sorry. Why the fool?"

"Because I wanna eat continents and sniff stars."

"You like traveling?" I said.

"I like to tumble through life, blind as fate."

"And spraying my poor man-brain with cryptic revelations?"

"Hold up that membrane. It'll shield you from the spray," Liene said.

I glimpsed a tongue on steroids, hiding, poking, almost shy behind a skirt made of teeth. It shuffled words in peculiar order, and seemed so strong, maybe from old years of lifting cocks and clits.

"Flip my words like them tarot cards, yeah?"

"You certainly know how to bruise with them," I said.

"Aww don't be like that, daddy."

A siren cry raced outside on urban veins. People dying. Undying if saved. The speed of luck. Desperate minds ruled these wasted streets. I rented bodies here. Home to me or other fat wallets.

"Tell me about Boomerang. Who is he to you?"

That name fell from my lips, worn and ugly. Something in her face changed. I clocked emotions dressed in secrets I did not know. Like his name was a severed limb she still felt. A phantom pain.

"Exactly that—he's my Boomerang."

"What do you mean?"

"I keep throwing him away, but he always returns."

"And he didn't return this time?"

More beer vanished down her throat, along with unvoiced answers. She spoke in blinks, projecting letters on a blank heart. I breathed in a well-guarded excavation site. Not even God knew what was buried inside that pale core. I had to dig. My tongue, my shovel.

"What else?" I said.

"A fellow Czech. We worked together."

"Maybe he returned home, rather than to your hands."

"Nah, he liked to stay close."

"Your boyfriend?"

"My plaything."

I prayed for basket case fluency. How much did he weigh on her scale of feelings?

More sirens punched through midnight wind. That noise was a vaccine against sympathy.

I wanted to be the stamp on a postcard from hell. Let them die for once.

"Why do you want him found?"

"I'm bored without his obsession."

"You got him eating out of your hand, huh?"

"Months of training."

"And you think I can locate him how?"

"Don't play stupid. It doesn't suit you."

"What?"

"Katerina said you know this city's every stain."

Her gumption sliced through me, sharper than hate. It seemed that reputation bounced fast between stains. I was mothered by greed, selling pleasure in all skin tones—eyes always calculating sums in flesh.

She waited, mouth suspended on a thread my words could pull in any direction.

"Maybe I can ask around for you."

Liene's face relaxed. "Good. That's all I want. I'll text you his photo and address."

"Presuming I find this bloke. Then what?"

"Find him first. Then we'll talk rewards."

I raised my beer-free bottle. "Liquid rewards?"

She searched and found dirty clues hanging from my lips. I thought about chance and her womb, where unborn fantasies still grew.

"I promise to feed you red and gold from the tightest pink, daddy."

I stumbled through the door, hearing familiar shadows. My place was a minimalist's bible. A sad mattress washed in booze, and woman's spit swallowed the room. Charity-bought clothes and discarded dreams lived on the floor.

Half-brothers in glass castles loved to poison me. I ate sardines from a tinned sea of oil, chewing chapters by candlelight.

I felt a little quake in my pocket. *B wit u soon. Kat xx.*

She spoke three languages. I only spoke in redheads.

More texts. Boomerang's arresting visage now hung in my phone gallery. His onyx eyes wrote on me like a ballpoint pen. Maybe he shared memories with tortured elephants. A double knock.

"That bitch is lying, yeah. I never said nothing."

Katerina was higher than a Boeing 747. I brought her down fast. She crashed somewhere between my hell and mercy. Blood always made her prettier.

"Tell your nose to stop trespassing in my business, or I'll cut it off."

I fed her hundred-calorie threats twice a week to keep her fear slim. She digested fast.

I ran my thumb across her lips, a red bank taking cash printed on sin. They earned triple digits in a single night.

"P-please. She was only askin' round."

"You give heads, not information," I said. "How do you know her?"

"She paddles coke in the docks, man. Good shit."

Her hunger meditated on the sardine grave. Inside, they spooned like half-eaten criminals. I heard their prayers down in my belly. Twice drowned souls skipping across clouds heard them, too.

"You eaten anything today? Excluding pussy?"

The apple belonging to Adam, and stolen by her throat, jounced beneath freckled skin. A strange vision. I thought about tumorous pigeons in saliva rain.

"I had soup." Katerina's eyes spun away from mine.

I whistled. A ticket to her meal. Greedy hand, a veiny elevator, rose to her mouth. Teeth split oiled bodies, painting her lips with the color of fish breaths. She sucked on murdered strength, one by one.

"I hope your tongue will step beyond the canned border."

"I like living on cans, man."

"Or in cans," I said.

My old bladder forecasted wet warnings again. Thirteen steps to the bathroom. A day of my birth. Maybe death. I pissed away blood, and some anger, too. I had no mirrors. They told unpleasant truths about misspent hours.

She dug glued-on nails in the skin of my carpet. Punters paid more for dirty habits.

"You gonna find her little boyfriend, then?" Kat said.

Silence. My roommate shuffled dust in the corner.

Kat was long gone when I listened to blind thoughts scratch at the walls. They said I slept with a fire ant once because she marched through my deepest wrinkles. Bones also spoke against me.

I jabbed words fast. *Found Boomerang. Meet in dockyard @ midnight.*

She lit up my key to the world with one breath. *See u there – L xxx.*

I smuggled lies in Moon's fading mouth, and watched stars choke on their own signs. The gate played games with guessing shoe sizes. I pushed away the pivoting leg born in cement. Eyes that drank from every ocean greeted me. I felt rich salt beneath them, rubbing on the poor thing beating in my chest. She still wore same colors as lung cancer.

"The kingpin of love…"

"...looking at his dream empire," I said.

Veneer commando stood guard behind her smile. I bribed with expensive words—my only wealth. Maybe she'd surrender her body, if the figure curved far enough.

"Glad to be part of it."

Liene hugged me. Her heart laughed when cruel love hammer struck—but I sensed weakness in iron storm. That flame hair always burnt my face with want.

"You okay?" she said.

"I want to sleep with your hair. In my bed and in my grave."

"Baby."

Her tongue was a charging bull. Maybe a Siamese twin, stuck to mine forever. I hoped. Our kiss carved coordinates on God's ribcage. It was that sharp. I felt my wood drift on his blood.

"Do I taste good under a different moon, daddy?"

She remembered my words and the scent of knowledge. The water coughed jealous rings served on a wet plate. I only heard her incoming tide.

"Let's sit on that ugly bench's face." Liene pointed.

I parked unfamiliar touch on her thigh, staying close to that little heat bunker.

"You caught my Boomerang?"

"I heard whispers from the winds he travelled on." I rubbed harder.

She ripped tactics from the belly of Switzerland. A neutral zone in a genital war—her body. No protest. Triangle sauna her only encouragement. But then asphyxiation splashed on me. Fat rope raped my neck meat.

I found no Boomerang. He found me.

Moss hands breached. They pulled our boat away from land barons digging for their worm wives. My eyes were abyss realms. I felt like a mouth bubble on the last of the Chernobyl dogs. Cloud people above wore catatonic halos. They even dropped saliva grenades.

"How do you know he's the one they want?" said a voice that always returned to her.

I heard a fat tongue caught in a lisp trap. Then foreign words bled around me.

We stopped on a mud bank, and the river pilot hands sunk again. The land of industrial brick giants, abandoned by father time.

Boomerang aimed his rifle at where my heart used to be.

"Move."

Footstep brigade somewhere. Then she played on my eyeball field.

Liene smelled like a transplanted aura. Maybe a half-hatched promise.

"I'm thirsty for red and gold from the tightest pink, baby."

"What?"

"I re-bridged your souls," I said.

"Quiet, old fool. We never met."

Lie-powdered bullets—a clean shot through my stomach. That pretense pulled me faster than threats.

We faced shutters inhaling rust. I watched her fingers preach to the shy lock hiding a steel eye. She was poison—a fume on sundown highway to locust city. A component of sin.

"Don't take it personally. There's truth in her estrangement."

His breath reminded me of scorpions.

"Meaning?"

"Meaning, she doesn't know who you are. That's why we're here."

Boomerang rifle-nudged me forward. He was hostage to love, even when his years wore gray. I had to be smarter than feelings.

We walked on future burial ground, *if* my luck died on a

cactus sword in a bone-thirsty desert somewhere. Stealing from Death's minibar, my last thought. Maybe.

"Stand right there, in that circle," he said.

Liene sobbed when a singing mirror reflected her body times five. Acid trips confused me less.

Daylight geometry. An optical illusion. Loki of the glass.

Boomerang read the wine list from my lips.

"You're not drunk. Do you see them?"

"What is she?" I said.

"An enigma."

Tiny emotional hands crunched up his face like old paper. I thought about upside down love bins, and that look falling out everywhere. I knew she slept inside ink pots. And how she stained minds.

"You in love, yeah?"

"With one of them," he said.

"What?"

"Five reflections, five personalities. When you die, they die, and only one remains."

"The one that loves you?"

Boomerang threw me a nod. In dreams, he wore her like a talisman. She was a delusion feeder. Hope in disguise. A red map to every heart.

"Why me?"

"Katerina is her sister. You introduced her to this sick trade. She hates pimps."

Sisters and their parasite politics. They manipulate faster than religion. I was the hooker God. The prayer, falling off a cliff.

Family. What a fat-rich word. I felt bloated, cremated.

"She came to me, man."

"It doesn't matter. Every year, we murder one of your kind. So is her ritual, her curse."

"Curse?"

"You really have no idea who she is, do you? Her mother was

a village Alkonost. She made people forget pain, forget grief. But it came with a price. They forgot everything they ever knew—to the point they never wanted anything again."

"I don't do witch lobotomy riddles, man. How do I fit into all of this?"

I was a dwarf in his intellectual rat eyes. A stain on a blunt instrument. That subspecies scorn, hiding between his wrinkles.

His shoulder rubbed against mine.

"Liene inherited those abilities. In reverse. The personalities her mother wiped flowed into her daughter during pregnancy. They inhabit her. Once a year, she forgets who she really is. The irony. Her mother made people forget. Now they make her daughter forget."

"And pimp-killing somehow pulls her back?"

"Yes. In pimp blood, she remembers hate. The hate you inspired by selling her sister's body."

I scoffed. "So? Katerina's only ability is to suck dick."

"Shut up. You will die tonight, and we will be reunited in your blood."

―――

Boomerang's rifle pointed at my head. I stared down the barrel, waiting to greet Brother Bullet—my only family. I imagined his kiss, warm on my cheek. Penetrating me, mouth-fucking me. His heat burning inside me as I bled out goodbyes. Then I thought of her.

"Can she do it? Please."

He coughed out cocaine anatomy. The place reeked of executioner's soap.

Liene stepped in. A ginger wall between us. His finger relaxed on the trigger. She unweaponed Boomerang and flipped 180. I winked hello. She dropped her aim, her gaze. My soul magnet ruined her flow since day one.

"Must take a lot of energy to look me in the eye," I said to the face that unbuttoned oceans.

Her cheeks were soaked red with casualties of internal war. I heard them dying.

Then she shot me—a glance. Eyes dark and loaded like cannons toasting midnight. Murder grew fat in the circus of her mind.

I dropped my eyelids. A terminal curtain for a crying world.

"Kill me."

The moment was elastic, stretching endlessly. Spirit outcasts pulled walls apart somewhere. I waited for gun hymns. They rang loud, and a body folded. Not mine.

"Sorry about the cheap theatrics."

In my sight bled a hornet. Liene. She made the ground look pretty. If beauty had a carcass, it was her. Those teeth. White tombstones carved by poem angels. A brand-new river, born today, passed through her mouth. The color of holy wine.

"What the fuck just happened?" I said.

Boomerang holstered his Beretta. He shook my hand, and wits.

"Relax."

"Who are you?"

"I rule the court you walk in."

"What?"

Every thought rang soprano-high. His eyes bought first-row tickets to my brain opera. I hid mine behind reason.

The situation reminded me of a clock with no hands. A white circle for a reversed death wish in a heroin vein somewhere.

Boomerang crouched above her face, almost studying her stillness.

"Katerina came to me, her words masquerading favors."

"Favors?" I said.

"Yes. She begged me to remove her interfering sister forever preaching reform. Katerina is a good earner, and she loves doing what she does, as you know. She also thinks very highly of you. So I designed a little ruse. Liene found you. You found me. And in the process of it all...you found yourself."

"I don't follow."

"When faced with death, you get to know a man. Character observation in trialing situations is something I relish. You react in a delicious way—and I like you, Tristan Grieves. I want you to come work for me."

"What about Liene?"

"My men will dispose of her. She's a nobody. Now come with me. Let's talk business."

Sentimentality was a defected animal. I dumped my feelings on the ground next to her body for someone else to find.

Boomerang lumped his arm around my shoulder. His feet moved, not mine.

"What are you doing?" he said.

"I'm taking her eyes, man. I want to meet them again at the bottom of a whisky glass."

Dear reader,

We hope you enjoyed reading *Soaking In Strange Hours*. Please take a moment to leave a review, even if it's a short one. Your opinion is important to us.

Discover more books by Erik Hofstatter at https://www.nextchapter.pub/authors/erik-hofstatter

Want to know when one of our books is free or discounted? Join the newsletter at http://eepurl.com/bqqB3H

Best regards,
Erik Hofstatter and the Next Chapter Team

Soaking in Strange Hours
ISBN: 978-4-82411-199-9

Published by
Next Chapter
1-60-20 Minami-Otsuka
170-0005 Toshima-Ku, Tokyo
+818035793528

31st October 2021

Lightning Source UK Ltd.
Milton Keynes UK
UKHW012149101221
395468UK00002B/106